Samuel French Acting Edition

Mirror of Most Value
A Ms. Marvel Play

by Masi Asare

Based on the Marvel Comics *by*
G. Willow Wilson, Adrian Alphona & Sana Amanat

D0061985

‖SAMUEL FRENCH‖

ISBN 978-0-573-70818-3

www.concordtheatricals.com
www.concordtheatricals.co.uk

FOR PRODUCTION ENQUIRIES

UNITED STATES AND CANADA
info@concordtheatricals.com
1-866-979-0447

UNITED KINGDOM AND EUROPE
licensing@concordtheatricals.co.uk
020-7054-7200

Each title is subject to availability from Concord Theatricals Corp., depending upon country of performance. Please be aware that *MIRROR OF MOST VALUE* may not be licensed by Concord Theatricals Corp. in your territory. Professional and amateur producers should contact the nearest Concord Theatricals Corp. office or licensing partner to verify availability.

Please refer to page 54 for further copyright information.

MARVEL SPOTLIGHT

Welcome, True Believers!

I'm so glad to have you join us and take your place amongst the legendary pantheon of Marvel heroes.

In the early 1960s, Marvel was a small, upstart comic book company introducing little-known characters like Spider-Man, The Avengers, Black Panther, and so many more that are household names today. It's been an exciting ride over the last 20 years as we've expanded from the printed page to animation, television, movies, and games. Complete and total world domination... well, almost. I've been fortunate enough to serve at Marvel during this time, first as Editor-in-Chief and now as Chief Creative Officer, and I firmly believe that our success in each of these mediums has come from our love for the characters and an unbridled excitement that we bring to each new challenge. That's why I can't begin to tell you how thrilled I am about Marvel Spotlight and your participation in it – it's going to be amazing to see you bring these stories to life.

Marvel Spotlight is an all-new way to experience some of the greatest heroes ever. But the best part is that we get to watch you interpret them in your own way as you expand the Marvel Universe into a whole new medium (yes, and *then* we can claim complete and utter world domination).

At Marvel we tell the stories of ordinary people doing extraordinary things and I can't wait to see what extraordinary things you'll bring to these stories. So now, if you'd indulge me, take a deep breath and say it with me, loud, so that they call down from hallowed halls of Asgard complaining about the noise: "Move over, Shakespeare! Take a seat, Chekhov! Here comes Marvel Spotlight!"

See ya in the funny books,

Joe Quesada
Chief Creative Officer
Marvel Entertainment, Inc.

WELCOME TO MS. MARVEL

In 2014, the all-new Ms. Marvel, Kamala Khan, entered the pages of Marvel Comics and made history. I was the original series editor on the book, having developed the character with G. Willow Wilson, Adrian Alphona, and Stephen Wacker. I knew we had something special on our hands, but I never expected the response: Kamala became a world-wide sensation almost overnight. The series received global media attention, became a *New York Times* bestseller, and went on to inspire a line of toys. How did folks get so excited so quickly? Perhaps it was because she was the first Muslim American to headline her own series. Or maybe it was because she was the first South Asian. Or possibly it was because she's from New Jersey. (Heroes can come from Jersey, okay?) Personally, I think it's something so much simpler.

As you get to know her, you'll realize Kamala Khan's story is one that transcends race, religion, gender, or any of the labels that tend to divide us. It's about forging your own path and making a difference with what you've been given. It's about stumbling toward goodness with a sense of heart and humor. It is no coincidence that Ms. Marvel wields "stretchy" powers. She stretches as far as she can, reaching across all our barriers, all the things that separate us, and she brings us in. She's a reminder of our similarities and our ultimate connectedness. She is all of us. Which means you have a hero within you too. As Kamala tells us, "Good is not a thing you are, it's a thing you do."

Sana Amanat
VP, Content & Character Development
Co-Creator, *Ms. Marvel* & Fan for Life

THE ORIGIN OF MS. MARVEL

High school student Kamala Khan grew up in Jersey City where she always dreamed of *rising* above her ordinary surroundings. Amidst her loving but protective family, she developed a passion for all things pop culture, including video games, science fiction... and especially super heroes.

One night, after finding herself enveloped in a cloud of the mysterious Terrigen Mist, she developed the ability to transform her entire body, and her life was changed forever.

Now, fighting crime on the suburban Jersey streets as Ms. Marvel, her shape-changing (polymorphic) abilities enable her to fight evil... while at the same time trying to maintain some semblance of a personal life. Just like her hero, Captain Marvel!

AUTHOR'S NOTE

It's easy to think that there's a "right" way to be a hero – to look like a hero, to have the right image, the right pictures, and the social media "likes" to prove it. I think so many of us feel this way – whether we're teens or so-called adults. And it's really easy to feel like you're doing things wrong, or that you'll never live up to expectations. The hero of *this* play, Kamala Khan, a.k.a. Ms. Marvel, is no exception. Coming from an immigrant background with strict parents and friends who push her to be the best version of herself, she sometimes feels like she's coming up short – even though she's got the costume and the powers that say differently. What I love about Kamala is that she doesn't give up – she keeps fighting to do the right thing. While I was writing, and reading every Ms. Marvel comic I could get my hands on, I definitely fangirled out about her courage and sense of humor through it all, and hope you do too.

Kamala's heritage is an important part of her identity as a super hero, and so I strongly recommend that the roles of Kamala and Ammi be played by female-identifying actors of color. I also recognize that this casting requirement might be challenging for some communities. I really struggled with the best way to approach this, but in the end decided it's most important to ensure as many theater artists as possible have access to this story. Whether *Mirror of Most Value* draws you in for the chance to showcase proud South Asian American identity (yes, people of color can be super heroes too!), or the chance to learn something new about a culture different from your own, I hope this play gives you the opportunity to find and celebrate your own powers in the theater.

Embiggen!

Masi Asare

CHARACTERS

THE TEENS

KAMALA KHAN – a.k.a. Ms. Marvel. Female identifying.

NAKIA BAHADIR – Kamala's best friend. Female identifying.

BRUNO CARRELLI – Kamala's other best friend and sometime crush. Male identifying.

GABE HILLMAN – Bruno's friend, the smooth guy. Male identifying.

ZOE ZIMMER – Kamala's kinda snotty classmate. Female identifying.

JOSH RICHARDSON – Zoe's boyfriend, the jock. Male identifying.

LEE – Josh's friend. Male identifying.

ALEX – Josh's friend. Any gender.

MICHAELA "MIKE" GUTIERREZ – Bruno's girlfriend, the new girl. Female identifying.

FANGIRL – Female identifying.

STUDENTS

THE ADULTS

AMMI – Kamala's mother. Female identifying.

MS. NORRIS – Physics teacher. Female identifying.

THE FAN FIC CHARACTERS

FAN FIC MS. MARVEL I, II, & III – Played in three different scenes by three different actors. Any gender.

BADDIES – REESE & **FLYNN** – Any gender.

DELI WORKER – Any gender.

CAT BURGLAR – Any gender.

REPORTER (1-2) – Any gender.

THIEF – Any gender.

FAN FIC ENSEMBLE

THE SUPER HEROES

CAPTAIN MARVEL – Female identifying.

IRON MAN – Doubled by the actor playing **JOSH**. Male identifying.

BLACK WIDOW – Doubled by the actor playing **ZOE**. Female identifying.

DOCTOR STRANGE – Doubled by the actor playing **LEE**. Male identifying.

Marvel Spotlight aims to create compelling plays with teenage protagonists who tackle real-world problems in a diverse society. Licensees are encouraged to approach casting in a way that values equal representation and inclusion while promoting conversation and respect. Characters designated "any gender" should be costumed to reflect the gender identity of the performers.

CASTING

Every effort should be made so that Kamala and Ammi, who are Pakistani American in this play and in the comics, are played by performers of color. For Ammi in particular, it's important that she not become a caricature. If the actor and director are not familiar with a South Asian accent, the role should be performed without any attempt at an "authentic" accent. The important thing is for the mother/daughter relationship to come through clearly in performance.

All other roles are open to performers of any ethnicity. The director and cast are encouraged to read at least *Ms. Marvel, Volume One: No Normal* of the comics to gain a sense for how these characters appear on the page, which could be a starting point for thinking about casting.

On the next page is one possible way to double (12 actors total, including Kamala).

Actor	Real Life	Fan Fic 1 (Scene One)	Fan Fic 2 (Scene Three)	Dream (Scene Six, Part One)	Fan Fic 3 (Scene Six, Part Two)
1	Kamala	Kamala	Kamala	Kamala	Kamala
2	Nakia	Ensemble 2	Fan Fic Ms. Marvel II	Offstage Voice	Ensemble 9
3	Bruno	Deli Worker	Passerby	Offstage Voice	Ensemble 8
4	Gabe	Reese the Baddie	Passerby	Offstage Voice	Fan Fic Ms. Marvel III
5	Zoe	Ensemble 3	Zoe	Black Widow/ Zoe	Passerby
6	Josh	N/A	Ensemble 4	Iron Man/ Josh	Passerby
7	Lee	N/A	Ensemble 5	Doctor Strange/ Lee	Passerby
8	Alex	N/A	Reporter	Offstage Voice	Thief
9	Mike	Ensemble 1/ Reporter	Cat Burglar	Captain Marvel	Ensemble 7
10	Fangirl	Fan Fic Ms. Marvel I	Ensemble 6	Offstage Voice	N/A
11	Ammi	Passerby	N/A	Ammi	Passerby
12	Ms. Norris	Flynn the Baddie	Passerby	Offstage Voice	Ms. Norris

SETTING

Kamala's bedroom; the streets of Jersey City; a physics
classroom and a hallway at Coles Academic High School

TIME

Present

SCENE ONE
Kamala's Bedroom/Streets of Jersey City

(A window, ajar. Sounds of traffic, honking, sirens... the city at night. On the walls are super hero posters, including a big poster of Carol Danvers – Captain Marvel. Outside the window, rustling sounds of shaking branches.)

KAMALA. *(offstage)* Ooof. Ouch! Ugh.

(A tree branch springs. Thwack.)

Don't even think about it, tree. *(throws a leg over the windowsill)* If I can take burglars and bad guys, I can take you. *(climbs into the room, pulls on a sweater over her Ms. Marvel costume)* Tonight was my best fight ever! I'm sure it's all over the news by now: "Ms. Marvel, Jersey City's new local hero!" *(opens her laptop, pause)* How did this *not* make the news? *(a new idea)* What about on my favorite fan fiction site, freakingawesome.com? I bet there's a ton of fan fiction about me by now... Nothing?? How can I be a super hero with no fans? Well. Like they say... You want something done right? Do it yourself.

*(**KAMALA** starts typing. Text projected/sign or voiceover: "MS. MARVEL SAVES THE DAY AGAIN AND IT'S SUPER AMAZING." She reads as she types.)*

"It was late at night and there was a shakedown going down at Jersey City Deli..."

*(Lights shift. Elsewhere, **REESE** and **FLYNN** – the **BADDIES** – face a **DELI WORKER** who shrinks from them in fear.)*

1

DELI WORKER. Listen... I can get you more money next week. It's just, my mom got sicker. And hospital bills are expensive!

(**FAN FIC ENSEMBLE** *enters, passing by.*)

REESE. Not my problem. Pay up!

DELI WORKER. I'm begging you! I'm the only one who can take care of my mom!

REESE. (*pulls out a weapon*) Stop yelling!

FLYNN. (*pulling out a weapon too*) Yeah! Stop yelling!

ENSEMBLE 1. Look! They have weapons!

ENSEMBLE 2. Oh no! We're all going to die!

ENSEMBLE 3. Someone saaaave us! Heeeelp!

(**FAN FIC MS. MARVEL I** *enters.*)

FAN FIC MS. MARVEL I. Hold it right there!

REESE. Um, who are *you*, exactly?

FAN FIC MS. MARVEL I. Ms. Marvel, of course.

(*The* **ENSEMBLE** *freezes.*)

(*to* **KAMALA**) Did you want to take this speech? I mean, since you're me. Or... since I'm you, in this fan fiction you're writing.

KAMALA. (*"This is so cool!"*) Yeah, you're my first fan fic *doppelgänger*! (*calming down*) No, it's fine. You can have the speech. The first half, anyway.

FAN FIC MS. MARVEL I. Cool.

(*The* **ENSEMBLE** *rewinds the scene a bit.*)

REESE. Um, who are *you*, exactly?

FAN FIC MS. MARVEL I. Ms. Marvel, of course. Patrolling the streets just like I've been doing every night these past six weeks. Ever since that weird Terrigen Mist flooded the city and I got these cool polymorphic powers.

KAMALA. (*typing*) "And I don't get why more people don't know about Ms. Marvel. So for everyone reading this on freakingawesome.com, she is a freaking awesome super hero and deserves to have more fans."

FAN FIC MS. MARVEL I. *(to* **KAMALA***)* That's a little much. No?

KAMALA. *(To* **FAN FIC MS. MARVEL I***)* I'm working like crazy to protect this town! And it's hard keeping up with school and hiding my secret identity from my family. But...

FAN FIC MS. MARVEL I. You don't want to sound desperate.

KAMALA. Right. Delete delete delete. "For everyone reading this, you'd best believe no one messes with Jersey City."

> **(FAN FIC MS. MARVEL I** *gives* **KAMALA** *thumbs up and turns to the* **ENSEMBLE,** *which comes back to life.)*

FAN FIC MS. MARVEL I. Not on my watch!

DELI WORKER. It's Ms. Marvel!

ENSEMBLE. She'll protect us! She'll protect us all!

FAN FIC MS. MARVEL I. *(to the* **BADDIES***)* You can't just threaten an innocent deli worker person.

REESE. Oh yeah?

FLYNN. What are *you* gonna do about it?

FAN FIC MS. MARVEL I. Glad you asked! I have my methods. *(stretching out her hands, commanding them)* Embiggen!

> *(Assisted by the* **ENSEMBLE, FAN FIC**
> **MS. MARVEL I***'s hands become two giant fists,*
> *which she aims at the* **BADDIES***.)*

FLYNN. Jeez, Reese. I thought you said this town had less freaks than New York.

FAN FIC MS. MARVEL I. I'm giving you one last chance to run away, only because I'm a generous person!

REESE. Forget it, lady! We came to beat up this loser and that's what we're going to do!

FAN FIC MS. MARVEL I. Well, I gave you the option.

> **(FAN FIC MS. MARVEL I***'s giant fists pummel the*
> **BADDIES** – *possibly in slow motion.)*

BADDIES. *(ad lib)* Ack!/Oof!/Ow!/Hey!

FAN FIC MS. MARVEL I. Had enough?

FLYNN. Stop! Please!

REESE. We'll be good, we promise!

FAN FIC MS. MARVEL I. I should hope so. And I think there's someone you owe an apology to.

> (**FAN FIC MS. MARVEL I** *gestures to the* **DELI WORKER.**)

FLYNN. What is this, third grade?

FAN FIC MS. MARVEL I. What was that?

BADDIES. Sorry!!

FAN FIC MS. MARVEL I. Good. Now get lost.

> (**BADDIES** *scurry away and exit.*)

DELI WORKER. I can't thank you enough, Ms. Marvel! Please accept this small gift for all you've done.

> (*The* **DELI WORKER** *hands* **FAN FIC MS. MARVEL I** *a small paper bag.*)

FAN FIC MS. MARVEL I. What's this?

DELI WORKER. A snack.

FAN FIC MS. MARVEL I. A snack?

DELI WORKER. I heard that the famous Ms. Marvel likes to eat gyros to restore her super powers after fighting crime.

KAMALA. *(opens an identical paper bag)* That is so true.

> (**KAMALA** *pulls a gyro out of the bag and takes a giant bite. In the fan fic scene,* **FAN FIC MS. MARVEL I** *accepts the gift.*)

FAN FIC MS. MARVEL I. Why thank you, Deli Worker Person.

DELI WORKER. Hip hip...

ENSEMBLE. Hooray!

DELI WORKER. Hip hip...

ENSEMBLE. Hooray!!

> (*The* **ENSEMBLE** *turns to the audience, with overdramatic "narrator" voices.*)

ENSEMBLE 1. And once again, Ms. Marvel easily defeated the shadiest of criminals.

ENSEMBLE 2. The crowds cheered in great celebration...

ENSEMBLE 3. ... joyous and forever grateful...

DELI WORKER. Hip hip...

ENSEMBLE. HOORAY!!!

> (**FAN FIC ENSEMBLE** *exits, cheering, with* **FAN FIC MS. MARVEL I.** *Lights shift.*)

KAMALA. *(mouth still full)* "... grateful for her courageous efforts in service of humanity." And... posted! I can't believe I'm a genuine, actual super hero. *(looking at the poster on her wall)* Just like you, Captain Marvel! *(noticing something on her laptop)* Ooh! I'm on the news! And isn't that Josh from school?

> (**JOSH, LEE,** *and* **ALEX** *enter with a* **REPORTER.**)

REPORTER. And you witnessed tonight's events, young man?

> (*The* **REPORTER** *holds the microphone up to* **JOSH.**)

JOSH. Yeah, I was there. I saw the whole thing, me and my friends. It was pretty tame. Just a few jokers out for some laughs. Then this crazy woman showed up in a costume...

REPORTER. Ms. Marvel.

JOSH. Ms. who? Never heard of her. Seemed like she had no idea what she was doing. She had these giant hands, it was pretty weird, and she kept tripping over them. Then this one time she walked into a glass window by accident.

> (**JOSH, LEE,** *and* **ALEX** *laugh.* **FAN FIC MS. MARVEL I** *enters, listening.*)

LEE. What did she think, that she could phase through walls like Vision?

ALEX. Yeah, that takes *actual* super powers.

LEE. Her only power was like weirdness.

JOSH. It was hilarious.

(**JOSH** *laughs harder.*)

KAMALA. No, it wasn't like that!

FAN FIC MS. MARVEL I. *(to* **KAMALA***)* This is not at all how you told it.

(**JOSH** *keeps laughing.*)

KAMALA. *(to* **FAN FIC MS. MARVEL I***)* He's got it all wrong!

JOSH. Finally, everyone got so freaked out by her... they just went away. And that's about it.

(**JOSH, LEE,** *and* **ALEX** *exit.*)

KAMALA. No, that's not how it went down!

(**FAN FIC MS. MARVEL I** *exits.*)

I was *heroic.* I really was!

(**AMMI** *enters* **KAMALA***'s bedroom.*)

AMMI. Kamala, what is all this noise?

KAMALA. Just... homework, Ammi.

AMMI. What kind of noisy homework do they give you that keeps you up to this hour?

KAMALA. I'm almost done, I promise. I just wanted... extra credit.

AMMI. *(looking over* **KAMALA***'s shoulder)* Extra... what is this? Who runs around town dressed like that?

KAMALA. It's Ms. Marvel, Ammi. The super hero. She... she saves people.

AMMI. Someone should save her from that outfit. How must her mother feel, a daughter running around town in that skimpy clothing?

KAMALA. Her outfit is cool! Whatever, you wouldn't understand.

AMMI. I understand it's time for less "extra credit" online surfboarding and more sleeping in your bed.

KAMALA. But I just—

AMMI. No excuses. It's late, *beta.* Don't keep us all awake.

(**KAMALA** *sighs.*)

KAMALA. Fine. Goodnight, Ammi.

(**AMMI** *exits.* **KAMALA** *closes her laptop, dejected.*)

SCENE TWO
Physics Classroom

(The next day at Coles Academic High School. **BRUNO** *and* **JOSH,** *and* **ZOE** *and* **GABE,** *are at work in pairs, along with* **LEE** *and other* **STUDENTS.** **NAKIA** *is working alone.* **MS. NORRIS** *walks around helping* **STUDENTS** *on their projects.)*

JOSH. Bruno, my man. I'm pretty sure we attach this here.

BRUNO. Yeah, I'm pretty sure we don't.

JOSH. Really? 'Cause it looks like it goes here.

BRUNO. Yeah, no.

ZOE. *(waves hand aggressively in the air)* Ummmm, excuuuuse me, Ms. Norris!

MS. NORRIS. Listen up, everyone. The clock is ticking! Only two more days to finish up these science fair projects. And some of this work is... *(looking around the room)* disappointing at best.

ZOE. *(high-intensity hand-waving)* Helloooo, could we get some help over here?

GABE. Chill, Zoe, we've got this.

ZOE. But the springy things aren't springing right. Ugh.

*(**KAMALA** dashes in.)*

MS. NORRIS. Late again, Kamala? This is becoming a bad habit.

ZOE. Ms. Norrrisss!

*(**MS. NORRIS** goes to help **ZOE** and **GABE.** **KAMALA** sits down next to **NAKIA.**)*

NAKIA. Did you get my texts?

KAMALA. What? Yeah.

NAKIA. So what do you think? About the rally on Friday?

KAMALA. Nakia – I don't have time for that.

NAKIA. Why? What's so important?

KAMALA. I have stuff to do.

MS. NORRIS. *(to all* **STUDENTS***)* Let's focus here!

NAKIA. *(to* **KAMALA***)* What do you mean, you have stuff to do?

KAMALA. My mom needs help around the house. With... cleaning out the... closets.

NAKIA. And you can't get out of it? The Kamala Khan I know would stop at nothing to ditch housework.

KAMALA. *(not that convincing)* I tried.

NAKIA. You've really changed.

KAMALA. My mom was really, um, insistent. *(back to the science project)* Does this circuit look right?

NAKIA. Kamala. This is *exactly* the point of the rally for global female education. Do you know how huge the gender gap is for school attendance? There are fifteen million[*] girls in the world that are not in elementary school right now. And because of what? Housework! And stupid gender expectations! It's up to us to fight for change. Don't you see that?

KAMALA. I *do* want to fight for change.

NAKIA. There's so much injustice in this world. We have to stand up for what's right.

KAMALA. I get it! I'm trying to make a difference—

NAKIA. But you're just lost in your own little dreamland. You're not... you're not mad at me, are you?

KAMALA. Of course I'm not mad at you.

NAKIA. Because I just get the sense that you're avoiding me lately.

KAMALA. It's been a busy week.

NAKIA. I thought we were best friends. And you keep ditching me and Bruno. He seems kind of down about it, to be honest.

---

[*] UN Women, "SDG 4: Ensure inclusive and equitable quality education and promote lifelong learning opportunities for all." UNWomen.org. Should this number change, feel free to alter Nakia's line to reflect the most up-to-date statistic.

(KAMALA *and* NAKIA *look at* BRUNO, *who is trying to keep* JOSH *from destroying their project.*)

BRUNO. Josh! Just – don't. I've got this.

JOSH. Whatever you say, Bruno.

BRUNO. You seem kinda distracted anyway.

JOSH. Yeah, I'm still thinking about that girl from last night.

BRUNO. Stop. I do not want to hear about your extracurricular activities.

JOSH. Aw no, man, I mean Ms. Marvel.

BRUNO. *(looks up sharply)* What? What about Ms. Marvel?

JOSH. I caught her in action last night. What a joke! They let anyone wear a super hero outfit these days.

LEE. *(leans in)* Remember when she walked into that window?

(JOSH *and his* FRIENDS *laugh loudly.* KAMALA *overhears and focuses intently on her project.* BRUNO *looks back and forth between* JOSH *and* KAMALA.)

JOSH. She wiped out, man! Trying to break her fall with those giant hands! It was hilarious.

BRUNO. You find it funny to see other people in pain?

JOSH. Bro, you should have seen it. Hi. Larious.

BRUNO. I'll be right back. Don't break anything.

(BRUNO *walks over to* KAMALA.)

Hey.

KAMALA. *(unfriendly)* Hey.

BRUNO. Are you using all these solar panels?

KAMALA. No.

BRUNO. I just need a couple more. Do you mind if I—

KAMALA. Fine.

BRUNO. Um, thanks.

KAMALA. Surprised you're willing to accept my help, for once. But whatever... it's fine.

NAKIA. What is with you two? Bruno, talk some sense into her. She said she's not coming to the rally.

MS. NORRIS. Less talking, more science-ing!

NAKIA. *(to* **BRUNO***)* You'll be there, won't you?

BRUNO. Of course. You're making a speech, right?

KAMALA. *(to* **NAKIA***)* You are?

NAKIA. See? You never listen! I've been talking about this for weeks: "Equal Rights to Equal Education"! *(to* **BRUNO***)* Something is wrong with her. Seriously.

BRUNO. *(to* **KAMALA***)* You're not sick or... or hurt, are you?

KAMALA. I'm fine! I wish you both would quit acting like I'm a three-year-old. You're worse than my mom!

BRUNO. *(to* **NAKIA***)* I'll be at the rally on Friday. Mike made this amazing sign. She's really excited. You can count on us.

KAMALA. Great! You and Mike can have a great time. I already have plans.

NAKIA. Just ignore her.

BRUNO. It's cool. Mike and I will definitely be there.

*(***BRUNO*** goes back to his lab table.)*

KAMALA. Mike this, Mike that. See? He has new friends now.

NAKIA. I don't think Mike is just a "friend." *(realizing)* Ohhh... I see what this is about!

KAMALA. What?

NAKIA. Are you jealous?

KAMALA. Why would I be jealous?

NAKIA. You are! I can't believe I didn't realize this! It's so obvious. You're jealous of Bruno's girlfriend!

KAMALA. Bruno has a girlfriend?

NAKIA. Mike! Michaela... you know, the new girl?

KAMALA. They're dating? Bruno and her? Mike?

NAKIA. Nice try. Don't act all surprised. I didn't know you had a thing for him! I mean, the two of you were always really close, until whatever fight you had last month. But I didn't put it together.

KAMALA. There's nothing to put together. I've just been busy. I didn't even notice that they were—

NAKIA. Ha! It makes perfect sense. But listen to me, Kamala, you are a strong independent human and you do not need a man.

KAMALA. But I don't—

NAKIA. I know you've internalized all these messages from society that say otherwise, but I'm here to tell you that you are beautiful just the way you are. And courageous, and smart. You don't need some boy to tell you that!

KAMALA. Nakia. You've got it all wrong.

NAKIA. Let's just go out for ice cream after school, you and me. We can watch rom-coms if you want.

KAMALA. But you hate rom-coms.

NAKIA. Exactly. But I will hold back from pointing out the oppressive way that women are portrayed in those movies, the ridiculous idea of love at first sight, finding your soul mate just 'cause you spill coffee on him or trip over his dog's leash or lock eyes in a crowded room with perfect lighting, I mean seriously, how idiotic—

KAMALA. Yeah, you're really holding back.

NAKIA. I won't mention any of that. I'll watch and suffer in silence, if it makes you feel better. Really. 'Cause that's what friends do. *(funeral serious)* I'm here for you.

> *(The bell rings. **KAMALA** grabs her bag and begins to exit.)*

KAMALA. I've got to run.

NAKIA. Kamala? *(calling after her)* When are we meeting up?

> *(**STUDENTS** file out of class. **MIKE** enters.)*

MIKE. Hey!

BRUNO. Hi, Mike. How was French class?

MIKE. Oh, well, you know. It's been three weeks so I'm basically fluent now.

BRUNO. *(grinning)* I'd expect nothing less.

MIKE. We're still on for bubble tea after school, right?

BRUNO. Of course.

MIKE. Hi Nakia.

NAKIA. Hi. So, a question: On a scale of one to ten, where one is minor concern and ten is totally oppressive, how would you rate the following rom-coms...

BRUNO. You're watching rom-coms? No way.

NAKIA. I'm kind of helping Kamala with a project.

MIKE. *(looking around)* Is she here? Kamala? I can't believe I still haven't met her.

BRUNO. She's kind of busy these days.

NAKIA. Are any of these movies even slightly not sexist?

(**ALL** *exit together.*)

SCENE THREE
Kamala's Bedroom/Streets of Jersey City

(That night. **KAMALA** *climbs in the window, wearing her Ms. Marvel costume. She collapses, exhausted, opens the paper bag she has brought and pulls out a gyro and fries, which she tears into.)*

KAMALA. Mmmf. What a night! I was stealthy. I was sassy. I was super strong. Yesss! *(opens her laptop)* I killed it. I mean, no, I didn't actually kill anyone. (I would never do that! Come on!) But I killed it in terms of like—okay whatever. You know. *(tapping on laptop)* Time to check out freakingawesome.com... how many likes did I get? I'm sure by now... Wait. Not one single like? How is this possible? That was the perfect super hero story. *(picking at her fries)* I'm losing my appetite. Which never happens. *(sighing)* I'll just have to try again.

(Lights shift. Optional text projected/sign or voiceover: "JUSTICE BY MOONLIGHT, MS. MARVEL STYLE.")

"It was another typical evening in Jersey City. Pools of moonlight spilled through the streets..."

*(**FAN FIC ENSEMBLE** enters, using overdramatic "narrator" voices again.)*

ENSEMBLE 4. After dinner, families were doing their usual family stuff.

ENSEMBLE 5. Little children were going to bed, while screaming that they did not want go to bed.

ENSEMBLE 6. Passersby were passing by.

ENSEMBLE 4. And shady characters were, as always, being shady.

*(More **ENSEMBLE** members enter, creating a street scene.)*

ENSEMBLE 5. In a luxury apartment complex near Journal Square, one such character was up to no good.

(**CAT BURGLAR** *appears on a fire escape, carrying a bulging bag.*)

ENSEMBLE 6. But this was not their lucky night.

(**FAN FIC MS. MARVEL II** *enters. The* **ENSEMBLE** *freezes.*)

FAN FIC MS. MARVEL II. That's my cue, right?

KAMALA. Hey! My second fan fic *doppelgänger*! Looking good. *(all business)* Yeah. That's the cue. Hit it.

FAN FIC MS. MARVEL II. Awesome.

(**FAN FIC MS. MARVEL II** *strikes a pose. The* **ENSEMBLE** *comes to life again.* **KAMALA** *keeps typing.*)

What's that I see? Someone skulking on a fire escape?

(**CAT BURGLAR** *stuffs a handful of jewelry into the bag.*)

Highly suspicious. I'd better check this out. *(to her arms/legs)* Embiggen!

(*With the help of the* **ENSEMBLE, FAN FIC MS. MARVEL II** *grows long legs and/or arms that ribbon down/out across the fire escape. She reaches for the* **CAT BURGLAR***'s bag.*)

CAT BURGLAR. Hey! Stop it, you creep!

FAN FIC MS. MARVEL II. Do these jewels belong to you? I don't think so.

(**FAN FIC MS. MARVEL II** *keeps lunging for the bag and the* **CAT BURGLAR** *keeps dodging her. The* **ENSEMBLE,** *noticing the commotion, gathers in a crowd nearby.*)

ENSEMBLE 4. Look over there!

ENSEMBLE 5. What's going on?

ENSEMBLE 6. Is that Ms. Marvel?

(**FAN FIC MS. MARVEL II** *takes hold of the* **CAT BURGLAR***'s bag and they struggle over it.*)

CAT BURGLAR. Whatever. What are you, a weird-looking cop?

FAN FIC MS. MARVEL II. Ha-ha. Obviously you know who I am and you're intimidated by my super strength.

(**ZOE** *appears on the fire escape.*)

Zoe! I mean... young person, what are you doing here? Has this criminal threatened you?

ZOE. *(gushing, as the Zoe-in-Kamala's-mind)* Oh, thank God you're here, Ms. Marvel! I was *sooooo* scared!

FAN FIC MS. MARVEL II. I've got your back, defenseless citizen of Jersey City.

ZOE. I... I tried to stop this burglar from stealing my mom's jewelry but they were too fast and too sneaky.

FAN FIC MS. MARVEL II. I'm on it.

CAT BURGLAR. Yeah, I see you have bendy arms and all but I don't think that's going to get it done.

(**CAT BURGLAR** *breaks away and tries to make a dash for it but is stopped by* **FAN FIC MS. MARVEL II.**)

FAN FIC MS. MARVEL II. You can't run around sneaking into people's apartments and stealing things. It's just wrong.

ZOE. Oh, Ms. Marvel, you're *soooo* brave!

CAT BURGLAR. Ha! You fight like a girl!

FAN FIC MS. MARVEL II. I'm not using my full strength, just so you know, 'cause that would be unfair.

CAT BURGLAR. *(sneering)* As if.

FAN FIC MS. MARVEL II. Fine! You asked for it.

(**FAN FIC MS. MARVEL II** *rips the bag out of the* **CAT BURGLAR***'s grasp.*)

CAT BURGLAR. *(over-the-top grief)* Nooooooo!

(FAN FIC MS. MARVEL II tosses the bag to ZOE and pins the CAT BURGLAR's arms behind their back. FAN FIC MS. MARVEL II's arms/legs shrink back to normal size.)

FAN FIC MS. MARVEL II. *(to ZOE)* Your mom's jewelry is safe now.

ENSEMBLE. Hooray!

FAN FIC MS. MARVEL II. I'll take this thief down to the police station.

ZOE. My hero!!

FAN FIC MS. MARVEL II. It was nothing. Really.

ZOE. Please accept this string of precious rubies as a token of my gratitude.

FAN FIC MS. MARVEL II. Doesn't that belong to your mom?

ZOE. Yeah, but look how many she has – she won't even notice it's gone.

CAT BURGLAR. See?? You should have just let me take it.

FAN FIC MS. MARVEL II. *(to ZOE)* No, no, I was simply doing my job. Farewell, young citizen of Jersey City!

> *(FAN FIC MS. MARVEL II exits, with the CAT BURGLAR.)*

ZOE. Farewell, Ms. Marvel!

ENSEMBLE. *(ad lib)* Farewell!/You're the greatest!/We love you!/Goodbye!

ZOE. I'll never forget you!

> *(ZOE and the ENSEMBLE exit, still buzzing with excitement.)*

KAMALA. *(typing)* "And once again, the daring Ms. Marvel rose to the occasion and prevented a heinous crime from unfolding on the streets of her beloved city. A beacon of hope in this day and age, she—" Oooh, Google alert! I'm in the news?

> *(ZOE reenters with a REPORTER, who holds a microphone for her. This is ZOE as she really is, not as Kamala imagined her.)*

REPORTER. So you were on the scene tonight. Tell us, just what did you see?

ZOE. Honestly? I've never been so offended in my life. I was climbing up the fire escape to the window of my own home... *as people do...*

REPORTER. Uh, okay.

ZOE. I just went out to get some air, you know? Possibly my boyfriend happened to meet me on the roof, but is that relevant?

REPORTER. Well, no, I guess not. But do your parents—

ZOE. Anyway! I'm minding my own business, by the apartment where I *live*, and this costumed character mistakes me for a burglar! Me! The most un-burglar-looking person ever. Look at this hair. And my skin. Flawless, right?

REPORTER. Well, you *are* sixteen, so it's not that surprising.

ZOE. I'm just saying. Un-burglar-looking.

(**FAN FIC MS. MARVEL II** *enters.*)

FAN FIC MS. MARVEL II. *(to* **KAMALA***)* Is this how the story *actually* goes?

KAMALA. So I was confused for one tiny second! She looked really suspicious!

ZOE. Meanwhile, there *really was* a burglar stealing all kinds of stuff from my parents' bedroom and then this *person...*

REPORTER. *(prompting)* Ms. Marvel.

ZOE. *She's* Ms. Marvel? Wow. 'Cause I'm like *marveling* at how incompetent she was. The burglar almost got away...

KAMALA. But they didn't get away! I caught them, that's the point! *(to* **FAN FIC MS. MARVEL II***)* And that's what I put in the fan fic... just the important stuff.

ZOE. ... Isn't that what super heroes are supposed to be good at? Fighting crime? And then... *(starting to giggle)* Then she tried to take this flying leap – like she thought she was *Spider-Man* or something – and she fell off the fire escape!

(**ZOE** *convulses in laughter.*)

REPORTER. *(to audience)* Well, it was quite an adventure today in Journal Square Luxury Suites, as we've heard—

(**ZOE** *grabs the microphone again.*)

ZOE. *(still laughing)* It was so weird... these long arms and legs flopping all over. Ugh! I'm going to have *nightmares.*

REPORTER. *(grabbing microphone back)* And that's all we have time for.

(*The* **REPORTER** *exits with* **ZOE,** *who is still laughing/making vomit sounds.*)

KAMALA. Forget Zoe. It was a great fan fic story... How many likes did I get? Come on, come on...

(**FAN FIC MS. MARVEL II** *leans in.*)

Not a single one?

(**FAN FIC MS. MARVEL II** *walks off.*)

(calling after) You just have to give these things time, that's all! I'll work harder. I'll train. I'll get stronger. I'll fight smarter. I'll fight *more... (to the poster)* ... And be just like you, Captain Marvel. I'll show them all... show them just who I really am. *(yelling out the window)* Don't underestimate me, world!

AMMI. *(offstage)* Kamala, is that you screaming like a crazy person?

(**KAMALA** *freezes.*)

(to someone offstage) I know, I know, *meri jaan,* she should be asleep by now. Let me go check.

KAMALA. Oh crap.

(**KAMALA** *closes the window, jumps into bed, and pulls the covers up to her chin. Lights down.*)

SCENE FOUR
High School Hallway

(The next day.)

MS. NORRIS. Bruno, I know that you are friends with Kamala. Isn't that right?

BRUNO. Yes. I mean, kind of.

MS. NORRIS. Well, I'm worried that her science fair project still isn't done.

BRUNO. She's not the only one. A lot of us are still working.

MS. NORRIS. Yes, but you're on version 3.0 of your solar-powered plasma ball. Kamala, on the other hand—

BRUNO. She'll be fine. She's one of the top students in our whole grade.

MS. NORRIS. I used to think so, but I'm concerned. This is cutting it close.

BRUNO. I don't see what I can do.

MS. NORRIS. Sometimes a little peer pressure works wonders. You'll talk to her?

BRUNO. I can try, but... She doesn't really listen to me.

MS. NORRIS. I need you to rise to the occasion, Bruno. That's what leadership is.

BRUNO. Leadership?

MS. NORRIS. That's what we're doing here at Coles Academic High School – cultivating future leaders! Right?

BRUNO. Uh, I guess so.

(KAMALA enters.)

MS. NORRIS. Oh, here she comes now. I'll ask her myself. Kamala! About your science fair project—

KAMALA. I'll finish it in time, Ms. Norris. I promise.

MS. NORRIS. You've always been a top student. Is everything all right?

*(**BRUNO** lingers.)*

KAMALA. Yes!

MS. NORRIS. Everything okay at home?

KAMALA. Of course. I'm fine.

MS. NORRIS. I'm always here if you need to talk.

KAMALA. *(backing away)* Thanks, Ms. Norris! I'm good! I'll finish the project! Bye!

> *(**MS. NORRIS** exits. **KAMALA** goes to her locker. **BRUNO** looks around to make sure no one is listening.)*

BRUNO. Are you sure you know what you're doing, Kamala? I saw on the news you fell off a fire escape?

KAMALA. Yeah, so what? These are the hazards of the job.

BRUNO. But you don't have to take unnecessary risks.

KAMALA. It comes with the territory, Bruno. I didn't ask for these powers – you know that. But now that I have them—

BRUNO. No one said you should turn into some kind of vigilante overnight.

KAMALA. You want me to sit around and sit on my hands? My giant hands? I'm not going to do that.

BRUNO. That's not what I'm saying!

KAMALA. I have a responsibility to use my powers for good. I thought you understood that.

BRUNO. Yeah, but Kamala, it's just—

> *(**ZOE** and **JOSH** enter, crossing through the hall.)*

ZOE. It was unnatural, the way her arms and legs were all stretchy? Soooo *gross.*

JOSH. Definitely not normal. Gives you the creeps, right?

ZOE. And then when she fell off the fire escape! I couldn't help it, I almost died laughing.

JOSH. I can just picture it.

ZOE. She calls herself Ms. Marvel? More like Ms. Complete Disaster!

JOSH. Ms. Freaking Awkward!

ZOE. Ms. Total Hot Mess!

(JOSH and ZOE exit, still laughing.)

BRUNO. Just ignore them. But are you sure you're not overdoing it? You can't keep up this schedule. It's crazy.

KAMALA. Is this some kind of sexist thing, like some "I have to protect the girl" stupidness?

BRUNO. Kamala, you know I'm not like that. I've kept your secret. I trust you. I just... I worry about you.

KAMALA. Yeah, this is definitely sexist. Nakia would have a field day.

BRUNO. She doesn't know, does she? About you being Ms. Marvel?

KAMALA. Of course she doesn't know! She thinks I'm crushing on you, all lovesick because you're dating that other girl!

BRUNO. She what?

KAMALA. She thinks I'm jealous of Mike!

BRUNO. *(a little too fast)* But you're not, are you? I mean, you told me—

KAMALA. Of course I'm not. You and Mike – I think it's great. I hope you'll both be very happy.

BRUNO. It's not like we're getting married.

KAMALA. It's really none of my business, Bruno.

BRUNO. Kamala... I wish you would hang out with us sometime. Mike really wants to get to know you.

KAMALA. Yeah well, sure. Sometime.

BRUNO. You should come to the rally tomorrow.

KAMALA. I can't! I have too much to do!

BRUNO. Jersey City can get along without Ms. Marvel for one evening.

KAMALA. You don't understand! No one's taking me seriously! No one even knows who Ms. Marvel is!

BRUNO. Shhh! Do you *want* the whole school to find out?

KAMALA. *(quieter but still worked up)* And my mom is driving me up the wall! And my science fair project is a failure! And my best friend thinks I'm in love, and I'm *not*. And... and I've written this amazing fan fiction and no one's liking it and I don't have any fans!

BRUNO. Okay, you're a little on edge here, Kamala.

KAMALA. I'm not on edge! You try living your life like this! This is my normal! It's just that no one—

> *(NAKIA and GABE enter.)*

NAKIA. Kamala! There you are! I've been looking all over.

KAMALA. *(hurriedly, to BRUNO)* It's just that no one understands.

> *(KAMALA slams her locker shut and dashes off.)*

NAKIA. Where is she off to in such a rush?

BRUNO. Her mom needs her to, um, clean out the garage, I think?

NAKIA. Seriously? First it was closets, now the garage?

GABE. Her mom is kinda intense, you know. Whew!

NAKIA. I've been in that house a million times, and it does *not* need that much cleaning.

BRUNO. *(legit worst liar in the world)* That's what... um, that's what she told me. So. Yeah.

NAKIA. Hmmmph. My sweet-talking skills are pretty strong. I'll talk to Mrs. Khan.

GABE. Good luck with that. You're a brave woman. I admire that.

BRUNO. Well, Nakia, I don't know if—

NAKIA. *(hurrying off)* Kamala! Wait up!

> *(NAKIA exits.)*

BRUNO. —I don't know if that's a good idea. Crap.

GABE. You all right, Bruno? You look kind of shaken up.

BRUNO. Nah, I'm fine. It's just...

GABE. Girl problems?

BRUNO. No, me and Mike are cool. That's going really well, actually. It's just—

GABE. I've got time, man. I'm boycotting economics class, as a matter of principle. Sticking it to the one percent, you know?

BRUNO. *(still distracted)* It's just—Kamala—

GABE. Aha. It *is* girl trouble. Talk to the master.

BRUNO. My thing with Kamala is... I feel like she takes me for granted. We've been friends since like forever. She's amazing. But she doesn't always pick up on stuff.

GABE. Yeah? Go on.

> *(***BRUNO*** and ***GABE*** *find a spot to hangout away from the main hallway.)*

BRUNO. I mean, there's been times where I've been like, "Hey, I'm trying to make a point here," and she just bulldozes with her own agenda.

GABE. Like trying to make what kind of point?

BRUNO. So yeah, I had a crush on her! But she never really showed any interest, right? She has this, I guess I can say, this part time job... And she doesn't have a lot of time for other stuff. Or people. And you know, it's cool. It's cool. I support that, but I kinda had to put whatever kinda feelings I had for her, like put that to the side. Let it go. And we're still friends. But she... I don't know... it's just, I have a girlfriend now, and I get this vibe that Kamala is like a little jealous...?

GABE. *(beat, definitive)* Naw man, I don't get that vibe at all. Really.

BRUNO. *(not listening)* And it's weird, 'cause I asked Kamala out, and she said no! So I don't know why she would be coming back now... I mean she's not coming *back* but... Anyway. Like I said, I let it go.

GABE. Are you sure about that? Because you don't fully sound like a man who's let it go.

BRUNO. No, I'm over it! I am.

GABE. And you have a girlfriend now, right?

BRUNO. No, yeah, like... I mean, yeah. Mike, my girlfriend – she's incredible. Not that I'm comparing them, but, I don't think Kamala ever listens to me that much. She's always dashing out to do her own thing. But... I can talk to Mike about anything. She's really, I don't know, she's special, right? She's special.

GABE. Listen to me, Bruno. Don't get it twisted. Mike is the one you're with. *(like to a child)* Miiike.

BRUNO. No, I know.

GABE. Kamala and you are *friends*.

BRUNO. Right.

GABE. I do not get the vibe that she is any way whatsoever interested in you.

BRUNO. Really?

GABE. Cool. Glad we got that figured out. See you in physics, man.

>   (**GABE** *exits.*)

BRUNO. Yeah, thanks, Gabe. Thanks for listening. *(to himself)* I just hope she's safe. In a friend kind of way. That's all.

>   (**BRUNO** *exits.*)

SCENE FIVE
Kamala's Bedroom

(That night. **AMMI** *enters stealthily, verifying the room is empty.)*

AMMI. *(to the air) Ahcha?* So you're sneaking out again? Well, let's see if you like what is here for you when you sneak back *in,* Kamala Khan!

> *(***AMMI*** *dims the lights and stands, waiting, arms crossed.* **KAMALA** *climbs in through the window in her Ms. Marvel outfit.)*

KAMALA. *(exhausted)* Need. Food.

> *(***AMMI*** *jumps out at her.)*

AMMI. Is this how I have raised my daughter?

KAMALA. *(yelping)* Aaah!

AMMI. And what do you have to say for yourself?

KAMALA. Ammi! What are you doing, hiding in the dark?

> *(***KAMALA*** *grabs a sweater and pulls it on to hide what she is wearing as* **AMMI** *switches on the lights.)*

AMMI. Me? This is my house! I can stand wherever I want to stand. What are *you* doing, climbing trees and crawling through windows?

KAMALA. No, Ammi, the thing is—

AMMI. It's disgraceful! To think, my daughter!

KAMALA. I can explain—

AMMI. Is this why we raised you in this country, in the lap of luxury? To sneak out at night to see boys?

KAMALA. To do *what?* Are you kidding me?

AMMI. Oh, I know what you are up to!

KAMALA. I really doubt that.

AMMI. I know everything.

KAMALA. You do?

AMMI. *(meaningfully)* Everything.

KAMALA. *(panicking)* Ammi, please, I know I should have told you, but—

AMMI. Your friend Nakia was here today.

(*Pause.*)

KAMALA. *(processing this)* Nakia.

AMMI. You told her you were cleaning the house for me. Ha!

KAMALA. Well she might have misunderstood what I was, um, saying.

AMMI. That Nakia is a lovely girl. Trustworthy. And what is this you're telling her? Lies!

KAMALA. It's just that things are complicated, Ammi.

AMMI. *Sab jhooth*! All lies! I am ashamed of you, Kamala.

KAMALA. You don't understand!

AMMI. Enough. You are grounded.

KAMALA. But wait, wasn't I already grounded?

AMMI. And now you're *more* grounded. You go to school, you come straight home. That's it.

KAMALA. *(scrambling for a reason)* But tomorrow is... the science fair! And, there's this rally... this special event that Nakia is organizing. Tomorrow. I have to be there. For her.

AMMI. I don't know.

KAMALA. Science fair! That's basically school! And I thought you wanted me to hang out with Nakia... "lovely girl"? Right?

AMMI. Ah, why can't you be more like Nakia? Such a sweet girl.

KAMALA. Ammi, I promise, you won't have to worry about me. I'll be good.

AMMI. It's too late for arguing now. We'll talk in the morning.

(**AMMI** *turns to exit.*)

KAMALA. Ammi?

AMMI. What is it now?

KAMALA. I'm sorry I'm such a disappointment to you.

> (**AMMI** *pauses, reaches in, brushes back*
> **KAMALA**'s *hair from her face. It is a tender
> moment but* **AMMI** *won't let her daughter
> think she is soft-hearted.)*

AMMI. Don't try to make me feel bad for you. You can't get out of trouble so easily. No more talking. Go to bed!

> (**AMMI** *exits.* **KAMALA** *flops down on her bed
> and opens her laptop.)*

KAMALA. Please tell me someone liked my fan fic. Just one person who thinks I'm actually a super hero. After the day I've had. *(staring at the screen)* Not even one like? Not one fan?

> (**KAMALA** *closes the laptop and curls up in
> bed. Lights shift.)*

SCENE SIX
Dreamscape/Streets of Jersey City

(**KAMALA** *dreams. The sound of dhol drumming. The mood is stark and stylized. Super heroes are arranged in a tableau:* **CAPTAIN MARVEL, IRON MAN, DOCTOR STRANGE,** *and* **BLACK WIDOW. OFFSTAGE VOICES** *chant angrily. The chanting grows in intensity throughout the scene.*)

OFFSTAGE VOICES.
The foolish can dream
But the worthy are few!
The foolish can dream
But the worthy are few!

CAPTAIN MARVEL. Quiet! *(calling out formally)*
Aspiring hero, one whose dreams are great,
The worthy are few.
Present yourself, and we'll deliberate.

ALL SUPER HEROES. *(agreeing)*
The worthy are few.

IRON MAN.
Where is Ms. Marvel, will she show her face?
Has she the courage to accept her fate?
The worthy are few.

> *(The dhol grows louder and more intense.* **KAMALA** *rises from the bed.)*

KAMALA. Captain Marvel! And Iron Man, Black Widow, Doctor Strange...? You're all here! Am I dreaming?

> *(The dhol diminishes to a low rumble.)*

OFFSTAGE VOICES.
The foolish can dream
But the worthy are few!

DOCTOR STRANGE. Silence! *(looking at* **KAMALA**, *assessing)*
Day after day, and night by night, she fights.
But time turns swiftly, now the hour is late;
The worthy are few.

KAMALA. Are you talking about me? I'm worthy! I'm a
hero too!

    (The **SUPER HEROES** *begin to laugh eerily.)*

BLACK WIDOW.
What has she done, what honors has she won?
What strengths, what powers can she demonstrate?
The worthy are few.

KAMALA. But I'm a real super hero, why doesn't anyone
see that?

IRON MAN.
The strength of arms is easy to unleash...

CAPTAIN MARVEL.
Strength of the mind is power with more weight.

BLACK WIDOW. *(to* **DOCTOR STRANGE***)*
The worthy are few.

DOCTOR STRANGE. *(agreeing)*
She fails to seek this knowledge, she is lost.

CAPTAIN MARVEL & IRON MAN.
Her greatest efforts, at best second-rate!

BLACK WIDOW & DOCTOR STRANGE.
The worthy are few!

    *(***KAMALA** *backs away. The* **SUPER**
    HEROES *advance on her, closing in. Only*
    CAPTAIN MARVEL *hangs back.)*

SUPER HEROES. *(mocking, growing louder)*
Give up your dream, Ms. Marvel, all is lost.
You cannot join our ranks. Accept your fate!
The worthy are few.

OFFSTAGE VOICES.
The worthy are few!
The worthy are few!

(*Suddenly* **AMMI** *enters. The* **SUPER HEROES** *turn to stare at her.*)

KAMALA. Ammi! What are you doing here?

AMMI. I would like to recite for you from the poet Iqbal.

KAMALA. (*embarrassed*) Ammi, not here! This is super hero stuff. You wouldn't understand.

AMMI. Shhhh! (*to* **SUPER HEROES**)
"*Tu bachaa bachaa ke na rakh ise,*
teraa aaina hai vo aaina..."

    (**CAPTAIN MARVEL** *steps closer to listen.*)

"*Ke shikasta ho to azeez-tar,*
hai nigaah-e aaina-saaz mein."

CAPTAIN MARVEL. (*nods in agreement, then "translates":*)
"A mirror has most value when broken.
Give your true heart, let your pride dissipate."

AMMI. (*To* **CAPTAIN MARVEL**, *confidently*)
The worthy are few. (*places her arm around* **KAMALA**)
Look deeper. For my daughter's heart is great.

OFFSTAGE VOICES.
No!
The worthy are few!
The worthy are few!

    (*The* **SUPER HEROES** *start laughing, louder and louder.*)

BLACK WIDOW.
What has she done, what honors has she won?

    (**BLACK WIDOW** *steps into the light, revealing that she is* **ZOE**.)

KAMALA. Zoe?

ZOE/BLACK WIDOW. (*mocking*) She calls herself Ms. Marvel? More like Ms. Complete Disaster!

IRON MAN. Give up your dream, Ms. Marvel, all is lost.

    (**IRON MAN** *steps forward – it's* **JOSH**.)

KAMALA. Josh?

JOSH/IRON MAN. *(sneering)* Hi. Larious. Ms. Freaking Awkward!

DOCTOR STRANGE.
Unfit to be a hero, we decree!

> *(**DOCTOR STRANGE** steps into the light. It's **LEE.**)*

KAMALA. What is going on?

LEE/DOCTOR STRANGE. *(laughing)* Her only power is like weirdness!

> *(**ZOE, JOSH,** and **LEE** move toward **KAMALA,** menacing. **CAPTAIN MARVEL** puts an arm out, protecting her.)*

KAMALA. Stop!! I *know* this is a dream. I just know it. Get out! All of you! Get out of my dream!

> *(The **SUPER HEROES** start to glide away, except **CAPTAIN MARVEL.**)*

CAPTAIN MARVEL. "Give your true heart, let your pride dissipate."

AMMI. *(urgently)*
"A mirror has most value when broken…"

KAMALA. A mirror? But what does that even mean, Ammi?

AMMI. *(taps **KAMALA**'s laptop screen)* Is this the mirror that shows you who you are?

CAPTAIN MARVEL. Be yourself, Kamala. Tell it like it is.

> *(**AMMI** and **CAPTAIN MARVEL** exit. The lighting returns to normal.)*

KAMALA. Be myself?

> *(**KAMALA** goes to her laptop and begins typing. Optional text projected/sign or voiceover: "ALL IN A NIGHT'S WORK.")*

"It was a regular Thursday night in Jersey City…"

(FAN FIC ENSEMBLE MEMBERS 7, 8, and 9
appear. They speak sincerely.)

ENSEMBLE 7. And honestly, our hero was a little down.

ENSEMBLE 8. It had been a tough week.

(FAN FIC MS. MARVEL III enters.)

FAN FIC MS. MARVEL III. *(excited)* This is me, right?

KAMALA. *(low energy)* Hello there, *doppelgänger.*

FAN FIC MS. MARVEL III. Should I... strike a pose?

KAMALA. Don't bother. Just keep it simple.

(FAN FIC MS. MARVEL III returns to the fan fic
scene and walks slowly through the streets.)

ENSEMBLE 9. Try as she might, she just wasn't sure she was
making a difference to protect the city she loved.

(More FAN FIC ENSEMBLE members enter and
create a street scene.)

KAMALA. "But being a hero is not about how good you feel
or how glamorous you look when you're out to save the
world. It's about keeping on doing the right thing, no
matter what."

(MS. NORRIS enters, walking down the street.)

"When you see an injustice, and you have the power to
do something about it, you seize your opportunity."

(A THIEF comes up behind MS. NORRIS and
grabs her bag.)

MS. NORRIS. Hey! Give that back!

FAN FIC MS. MARVEL III. Ms. Norris? Oh no!

(The THIEF starts to dash off.)

MS. NORRIS. Stop! Thief! My handbag!

(FAN FIC MS. MARVEL III springs into action.)

FAN FIC MS. MARVEL III. Feet, embiggen!

(Assisted by the ENSEMBLE, FAN FIC
MS. MARVEL III grows giant feet and runs
after the THIEF.)

ENSEMBLE. *(ad lib)* Who is that?/Wow, her feet are huge!/
That's kind of weird./Do you think she'll catch him?/
Hey, I think that's Ms. Marvel!

> *(**FAN FIC MS. MARVEL III** catches up to the **THIEF**,
> but she trips over her giant feet and falls
> down. A few **PASSERSBY** go to help her.)*

THIEF. Ah-ha-ha-ha-ha! Nice work, Ms. Marvel. Just a
few *feet* from glory, am I right? Better luck next time,
ah-ha-ha-ha-ha!

> *(**FAN FIC MS. MARVEL III** snakes out a long
> arm.)*

FAN FIC MS. MARVEL III. Don't you know there's such a thing
as celebrating too early?

> *(**FAN FIC MS. MARVEL III** yanks the purse back.)*

THIEF. Hey! Give it back!

> *(Still sprawled on the ground, **FAN FIC
> MS. MARVEL III** aims a giant fist in the **THIEF**'s
> direction.)*

FAN FIC MS. MARVEL III. You really want to get into it with
me?

THIEF. Never mind. Forget it!

> *(The **THIEF** exits running. **FAN FIC MS.
> MARVEL III** stands up, feet and hands normal
> size again. The **ENSEMBLE** starts to disperse.)*

MS. NORRIS. Ms. Marvel, is it? Yes, I've seen you on the
news. I can't thank you enough.

FAN FIC MS. MARVEL III. No problem. It's my pleasure.
Really.

MS. NORRIS. Oh no, and you're injured!

FAN FIC MS. MARVEL III. Don't worry about it.

FAN FIC MS. MARVEL III & KAMALA. It's all in a night's work.

> *(Lights down.)*

SCENE SEVEN
Physics Classroom

(The next day. **BRUNO** *and* **JOSH** *are fiddling with their project.)*

JOSH. Bro, I really think this wire goes here.

BRUNO. That makes no sense.

JOSH. Hey, how come you're always shutting me down?

BRUNO. Okay, give it a try.

JOSH. Yeah?

BRUNO. Why not.

*(***JOSH*** attaches the wire. Nothing happens.)*

JOSH. Hmmm. I guess you were right, man. Or maybe over here?

*(***KAMALA*** runs in.)*

MS. NORRIS. Nice of you to join us, Kamala. Class is only half over.

*(***KAMALA*** hurries to join ***NAKIA*** at their lab table.)*

KAMALA. Sorry!

*(***NAKIA*** moves to make space, not saying anything.)*

Nakia. Talk to me.

(Silence.)

I know I haven't been a good friend recently.

(More silence.)

And I know you're mad at me.

NAKIA. I have a right to be mad. You *lied*, Kamala.

KAMALA. I didn't mean to—

NAKIA. But you did!

KAMALA. I know. I'm sorry. I'm really sorry, Nakia.

NAKIA. I just don't understand you, Kamala. I thought we were best friends.

KAMALA. We are!

(*Josh and Bruno's project suddenly lights up.*)

JOSH. Yesss!

MS. NORRIS. Nice work, both of you.

JOSH. We did it!!

BRUNO. (*smiling*) Yeah. Teamwork.

ZOE. Yay Joshie! You're so amaaaazing!

GABE. Zo, something's wrong with ours. It's not lighting up like it's supposed to.

(**GABE** *fiddles with the project in front of him and* **ZOE** *goes into hand-waving mode.*)

ZOE. Ms. Nooorrrrisss!

MS. NORRIS. Lord give me patience with these children today. After that run-in with a purse snatcher, I am worn out.

BRUNO. Wait, what happened, Ms. Norris? You were mugged?

MS. NORRIS. I'm fine, Bruno. Luckily that Ms. Marvel was nearby.

ZOE. Ms. Marvel? (*giggling*) What did she do this time?

MS. NORRIS. Her fight tactics were ingenious. She pretended to trip in the street. Fell flat on her face, on the ground.

(**JOSH** *and* **ZOE** *start to laugh.*)

But it was all a ploy.

(**BRUNO** *and* **KAMALA** *exchange a look.*)

BRUNO. I see. All a ploy.

MS. NORRIS. Because the thief was caught off guard when she made her move. And she got my purse back safe and sound.

BRUNO. Like you said, Ms. Norris... ingenious.

(**KAMALA** *smiles.*)

MS. NORRIS. I'm thankful she was there. *(goes to help* **ZOE** *and* **GABE***)* Now, what was your question, Zoe?

KAMALA. *(to* **NAKIA***)* But we *are* still best friends, Nakia.

NAKIA. Are you sure, Kamala? You're always distracted these days. You never pay attention to what's important to me. You're late to school all the time. You look like you haven't slept in a week.

KAMALA. You can tell?

NAKIA. Of course I can tell! I'm your best friend!

KAMALA. *(throws her arms around* **NAKIA** *in a huge hug)* We're still best friends! Yayyy!

NAKIA. *(fake grumpy)* Stop it! I'm still mad at you. Are you going to tell me what's going on?

> *(Pause.)*

KAMALA. It's a lot of things, actually.

NAKIA. I'm waiting.

KAMALA. Well, for one thing... you know what you said about me and Bruno?

NAKIA. I knew it!

KAMALA. It's not that I'm jealous, exactly. But... well, it's weird when friendships change, you know?

NAKIA. Adulting is awful. I plan to stay young forever.

KAMALA. I *want* to get to know Mike but what if it's awkward? You and me and Bruno, we've been friends for so long. Now we'll have to make extra space for her.

NAKIA. You should come to the rally after school. There's enough space for all of us.

KAMALA. Yeah, well, I'm grounded.

NAKIA. Your mom?

> *(***KAMALA*** nods and makes a face.)*

I'll talk to her.

KAMALA. You will?

NAKIA. Of course. You have to come.

KAMALA. *(back to the science fair project)* Now, if I can just get this thing to work right.

NAKIA. Yeah, this is supposed to be your specialty! What are we missing?

> (**KAMALA** *pokes at the project. Its lights flicker a bit and then go off.* **BRUNO** *lurks nearby.*)

BRUNO. I, um, I think you might need a different inverter.

KAMALA. Really?

NAKIA. Ohhhh. I see what you mean. Try this one, Kamala.

BRUNO. Yeah, I think...

> (**KAMALA, BRUNO,** *and* **NAKIA** *tinker with Kamala's project.*)

NAKIA. Hey! Look!

> *(The project clicks into gear, its solar-powered lights shining.)*

MS. NORRIS. Nicely done! And that's it for today. Pick up your projects this afternoon and see you all at the science fair!

> (**STUDENTS** *start to leave the classroom.* **MIKE** *runs in with a huge poster board sign for the rally.*)

MIKE. Bruno! Are you ready? Walk with me to English?

BRUNO. Oh, hey, Mike. Yeah. One minute.

KAMALA. Hi, I'm Kamala. I've heard so much about you.

MIKE. Hi! Me too! Nakia and Bruno talk about you all the time.

NAKIA. *(loud whisper, to* **KAMALA***)* I'm so proud of you!!!

MIKE. *(to* **KAMALA***)* Are you coming to the rally today?

> (**BRUNO** *puts his arm around* **MIKE**.)

BRUNO. She can't make it, but—

KAMALA. I'll be there.

NAKIA. You won't regret it, Kamala. We are going to change the world today.

MIKE. Yay! This is going to be so powerful.

KAMALA. Wouldn't miss it. I want to do my part.
(*to* **MIKE**) I like your sign, did you make that?

> (**NAKIA** *links arms with* **KAMALA** *and* **MIKE** *as the three of them start to walk off together.* **GABE** *comes up to* **BRUNO**.)

GABE. See, man? Everything works out the way it's supposed to.

BRUNO. Hey, I wasn't worried. I got my advice from "The Master."

GABE. I do what I can.

NAKIA. Wait till you hear my speech. Will you listen to me practice?

KAMALA. Whatever you need, Nakia. I'm here for you.

> (**ALL** *exit.*)

SCENE EIGHT
Kamala's Bedroom/Streets of Jersey City

(The completed science fair project is in view, with a ribbon on it. A sign from the rally leans against the bed. **KAMALA** *is putting on her Ms. Marvel costume. Ding! A sound from her laptop – she goes to look at its screen.)*

KAMALA. No way... My fan fic from last night got a like? Who is this? They commented? I have a fan!

(The **FANGIRL** *enters, a little shy. Maybe she is one of the Coles Academic High School students we have seen at various points earlier in the play.)*

FANGIRL. Hey. I just wanted to say, I love your fan fic. Because everyone always talks about heroes like they're so... put together. All shiny and beautiful, like the best versions of people. But the way you wrote about Ms. Marvel, well, I liked that she wasn't perfect. She seemed actually kind of ordinary! Like me. And it made me think... what you said about how you just have to do your best, even if you don't look graceful or smooth all the time? It made me think that the little stuff I do to try and make the world better, that little stuff counts too. Like there are more ways to be a super hero than I realized. So thank you. Truly. Can't wait for your next story!

KAMALA. Thanks for reading, Jcityfangirl. Ms. Marvel's definitely not perfect. No one is, honestly. But check back soon... I've got a bunch of new stories in the works!

*(***FANGIRL*** waves and exits.* **KAMALA** *strides to the window, and climbs out with purpose. Outside the window, tree branches bouncing. The sound of someone falling to the ground.)*

Ooof! Ack! Ouch!

(Sound of the dhol drumming, steady. **AMMI**
enters stealthily. She notices **KAMALA**'s *empty
bed and the window ajar. She shakes her
head and smiles knowingly before exiting.
The dhol turns into bhangra dance music.*
KAMALA, *as Ms. Marvel, appears on the
streets of Jersey City, running. Assisted
by the* **ENSEMBLE**, *she leaps up into the air,
one of her hands balled up in a giant fist.
Blackout.)*

End of Play

GLOSSARY

Below are explanations of the Urdu phrases, literary references, and less common words found on the page numbers in parentheses.

Ahcha (26): Urdu for "Oh, really?" Pronounced AH-chah.

Beta (6): In Urdu, an affectionate term parents use to refer to their child. Pronounced BAY-tah.

Bhangra (41): Energetic popular music and dance genre associated with urban South Asian diaspora communities; has roots in folk music of the Punjab region (northeastern Pakistan and northwestern India).

Dhol (29, 41): A large double-headed barrel drum popular in South Asia and featured in bhangra music; played with sticks and slung over the neck of the player with the help of a strap.

Doppelgänger (2, 15, 33): A German term for a ghostly counterpart, or someone who looks very much like another. Coined in 1796 by writer Johann Paul Richter in reference to German folklore that all living creatures have a spirit double who is invisible but identical to the living individual.

Ghazal (46, 48, 49): A form of poetry originating in seventh-century Arabia that traditionally invokes melancholy, love, longing, and metaphysical questions. Pronounced guzzle.

Iqbal (31, 43, 46, 47, 48): Muhammad Iqbal (1877–1938), poet and philosopher, born in British-controlled India (now Pakistan). Considered one of the most influential figures in Urdu literature.

Meri jaan (19): Urdu for "my darling." Pronounced MEE-ree JAHN.

Rising (VI): *Marvel Rising*, a Marvel Animation franchise, based on Marvel characters, including Ms. Marvel, Squirrel Girl, and America Chavez. Focuses on the

Secret Warriors, a diverse team of teen super heroes who join forces to protect the world from powerful threats.

Sab jhooth (27): Urdu for "lies." Pronounced sahb JOOT.

"Tu bachaa bachaa ke na/rakh ise, teraa aaina hai vo aaina..." (31, 46): A couplet from Muhammad Iqbal's *"Kabhi ai haqeeqat-e muntazar,"* a famous ghazal; the title translates to, "For once, O long-sought truth." For full translation and pronunciation of the couplet, see p. 56.

Urdu (42, 46): Closely related to Hindi, a language that originated in the Indian subcontinent. Spoken as a first language by more than 100 million people, it is the official state language of Pakistan and one of the official languages of India.

PRODUCTION NOTES

The following pages offer historical context along with design and performance suggestions to inform your production of *Mirror of Most Value*. For more tips and guidance on how to approach the Marvel Spotlight plays in production, visit MarvelSpotlightPlays.com.

Historical Background: Pakistan

The parts of the world now known as India and Pakistan were united until 1947 when, encouraged by British colonial rule, they were divided in a bloody, violent event that displaced over 14 million people. This "Partition" divided Muslim neighbors from Hindu ones and created the separate Muslim country of Pakistan. Religious differences aside, South Asian people from India and Pakistan (and their diaspora communities around the world) have much in common. For example, the music of Bollywood (from the film industry based in the city Bombay, also known as Mumbai, in India) has many similarities to the music of Lollywood (from the film industry based in the city Lahore, in Pakistan). In this play, and in the comics, Kamala and her family are Pakistani American.

Costumes

Hijab: Nakia wears hijab (a symbolic headscarf), which as her character in the comics reveals, is her personal choice to reflect her religious beliefs as a Muslim American. If the actor playing Nakia has never worn hijab, she and the director should consult with a Muslim woman who does about the correct way to wear hijab respectfully. For more information and to find resources in your area, consider contacting organizations like the Muslim American Society or the Islamic Cultural Center of New York.

Super Heroes: For Scene Six, keep the super hero costumes – for Captain Marvel, Iron Man, Doctor Strange, and Black Widow – as simple as possible, as these characters are seen only briefly. Avoid wigs and store-bought costumes, and instead approach your design creatively. Consider, perhaps, an abstract design to go along with the dream setting. Shirts or tunics in the heroes' colors and logos can clarify who these characters are without breaking your budget, while dramatic lighting can help sell any concept.

Props: Global Female Education Rally

Throughout the play, characters refer to a rally for global female education through dialogue and Mike and Kamala's hand-held signs. There also should be posters in Coles Academic High School hallways, e.g., "Rally for Global Female Education! Friday, 4 P.M." "Stand Up for Gender Equity," "This Is What a Scientist Looks Like" (with images of girls and women), "A Girl's Place Is with Her Textbooks," etc.

Staging: Fan Fic Sequences

The show functions as a kind of backstage drama in which Kamala appears as Ms. Marvel either just before or after her latest adventure. When she starts to narrate/re-imagine her super hero exploits as each "fan fic" she is writing, other cast members appear to take on the role of Ms. Marvel (as Fan Fic Ms. Marvel I, II, and III). To heighten the theatricality of these sequences, consider underscoring them with (over)dramatic instrumental music.

Ms. Marvel's super power of "embiggening" can be portrayed onstage in many ways, whether with shadow puppets and lighting, or with the Fan Fic Ensemble members producing and/or controlling elements such as inflatable boxing gloves, clown shoes, and ribbon or fabric for long arms and legs.

The two news segments following the fan fics (Josh and friends in Scene One, Zoe in Scene Three) can be staged live or as pre-recorded video.

Reciting Poetry: Kamala's Dream

Kamala's dream in Scene Six incorporates a couplet from *"Kabhi ai haqeeqat-e muntazar,"* a famous poem by Muhammad Iqbal in the Urdu language. Pronunciation and meaning of that couplet can be found in the chart below. In the dream, the super heroes' lines in English are loosely in the form of a ghazal, the same form as Iqbal's poem, and should be performed in a stylized way (think of how iambic pentameter is more heightened). For more information on Iqbal and ghazals, refer to the Glossary on pages 42-43.

ORIGINAL	PRONUNCIATION	MEANING
Tu bachaa bachaa ke na rakh ise	too bah-CHAH bah-CHAH kay nah ruck ih-SAY	Do not try to protect it against breaking
teraa aaina hai vo aaina	TAY-rah ah-YEE-na heh voh ah-yee-NA	because your mirror is the one
Ke shikasta ho to azeez-tar	kay shee-KAHS-tah hoh toh uh-ZEEZ-tuhr	that, if it were to crack
hai nigaah-e aaina-saaz mein	heh nuh-GAH-hay ah-YEE-na sahz mey	would be dearest in the eyes of the creator

BEYOND THE STAGE

Facilitating a productive rehearsal process isn't just about having clear rehearsal plans, it's also about meaningful engagement and ensuring the well-being of your cast. It's important your cast feels physically, emotionally, and artistically safe throughout the rehearsal process. The following pages include resources to help:

- In-Rehearsal Discussion Starters
- Rehearsal Exercises
- Post-Show Talkbacks

For best practices on stage combat and to ensure the physical safety of your performers, ideas on how to make the Marvel Universe theatrical, and additional exercises to connect to the world of comics, go to MarvelSpotlightPlays.com.

In-Rehearsal Discussion Starters

Throughout the rehearsal process, help your cast make deeper connections to the play and their characters using the following prompts:

- Kamala struggles to reconcile her sense of self with others' perceptions of her. Why do you think that is? How do you relate to this struggle?
- The play features a translation of a poem by the influential poet and philosopher Muhammad Iqbal. What do you think is the meaning of this poem? How does it connect to the title of the play, *Mirror of Most Value*?
- What motivates Kamala to fight crime in the beginning of the play? How about the end?

Rehearsal Exercises

The director's job is not only to helm the vision of the show, but also to assist actors in developing a bond as an ensemble, introduce them to the world of the play, and guide them to join the storytelling process. Below are a wide variety of exercises that will help with that. For even more rehearsal exercises, visit MarvelSpotlightPlays.com.

AN ENSEMBLE GHAZAL

Use this to: *help your actors work together to understand the use of ghazal in* Mirror of Most Value *and write one that represents the values of their ensemble.*

Share with your cast that a ghazal is a type of poetry composed of a minimum of five, and typically no more than fifteen, couplets that has origins in Arabic verse. The ghazal is a complex poetic form. However, this exercise focuses on two components: the ending of each couplet with the same word or phrase and lines of equal meter. In *Mirror of Most Value*, Scene Six features an English translation of the ghazal poem *"Kabhi ai haqeeqat-e muntazar"* by Muhammad Iqbal. In the play, the excerpt of this poem is used to explore the idea of self-worth and how someone demonstrates their value. Share with your cast that together they will create an ensemble ghazal for their rehearsal process.

As a group, brainstorm what you think makes a valuable cast member and write the answers on the board. Next, brainstorm a word or phrase that reflects who you are as an ensemble. Divide your cast into small groups. Each small group should be responsible for writing a couplet that describes an aspect of a valuable cast member. The only guidelines are that they should pull from the ideas generated by the ensemble and their couplet must end on the word or phrase the full group came up with at the beginning of the activity. After each group has completed their couplet, compile the couplets into one ensemble ghazal. If time allows, ask each small group to practice performing the ghazal in unison and add some gestures for a unison performance of the ghazal.

Apply to rehearsal: by incorporating the ensemble or small group reading of the ghazal at the top of each rehearsal. You can use this opportunity to experiment with student-devised blocking that you can utilize when staging Scene Six.

EMBODYING EMBIGGENING

Use this to: explore how to physicalize the process of embiggening with your cast.

Share with your cast that the super hero Ms. Marvel is known for her ability to embiggen different parts of her body, and that today they will explore how that may impact movement. Prompt your actors to move around the space as if they were walking down the sidewalk. Next, ask your actors to imagine that their feet are slowly swelling to double their normal size, then five times, and then ten times. As they move, encourage them to consider how the swelling may impact their ability to walk, jump, and kick. Ask your actors to return to their neutral walk, and then repeat this process with their hands and their arms. Gather your cast into a standing circle and reflect on the activity using the following questions: How would an enlarged hand, foot, or arm improve and/or hinder your ability to defend yourself from a villain? How could you theatrically illustrate these enlarged body parts on the stage?

Apply to rehearsal: by using this as a warm-up for the performers who play Fan Fic Ms. Marvel I, II, and III before blocking the scenes in which their characters embiggen, and by using ideas from the reflection in your staging of embiggening.

VALUING FAN FICTION

Use this to: connect to the character of a super hero super fan and understand the role fan fiction plays in Kamala's self-confidence.

Facilitate a discussion with your cast about the meaning of the phrase "fan fiction." Next, ask your cast to reflect on how they show appreciation for the celebrities and organizations they are fans of (e.g., e-mail, social media, etc.). Prompt your actors to step into role as their assigned character's super fan to write a fan fiction social media post in celebration of something their character does in the play. This post should be no more than 280 characters. Next, divide your actors into pairs and direct them to swap fan fiction posts. Partner A will step into role first as super fan and read Partner B's character fan fiction while Partner B steps into character and pantomimes the action happening in the post. Then they will swap, with Partner B becoming the super fan of Partner A. If time allows, ask each pair to share their fan fictions to celebrate the importance of each character in the story.

Apply to rehearsal: by reflecting, as a group, on the role of fan fiction in *Mirror of Most Value* using the following questions: Why does Kamala write fan fiction for her own super hero character? What is she looking to gain from the internet response? Who are actual fans of Ms. Marvel, and how do they show her their support?

Post-Show Talkbacks

Post-Show Talkbacks encourage audiences to forge deeper connections with your production. The following prompts can help start the conversation:

- What roles do family and cultural identity play for the characters?
- What strengths do the characters possess that aren't super human?
- Why, as a society, do we build up celebrities or icons? How does that influence our daily reality?

MS. MARVEL ORIGIN SKETCH

The following sketch introduces Kamala Khan as
Ms. Marvel as a way to promote *Mirror of Most Value*. It
can be performed anywhere that attracts an audience (the
cafeteria, for example) or filmed and posted on the school
or theater's website; it can even be played or performed
pre-show in order to familiarize your audience with our
hero. Additionally, you may also consider publishing The
Origin of Ms. Marvel (p. VI) in your program.

(**KAMALA**, *wearing a giant sweater, is at her
laptop, slurping a soda, and munching on
snacks.*)

NARRATOR. *(big booming voice, to the audience)* It was
late one evening on an ordinary, boring street in
Jersey City. And Kamala Khan was at home doing her
physics homework. Because she was one of those A+
students – good at school, not that good at fitting in.
An ordinary, boring teenager.

KAMALA. *(to* **NARRATOR***)* Hey! Hold on.

NARRATOR. It was true, however, that she read a lot of
comics. Like a *lot*.

KAMALA. Yeah, but who doesn't? Right?

NARRATOR. And she played way too many video games.

KAMALA. *(bragging)* This one time, I took down the entire
ring of space creature bandits in *Intergalactic Unicorn*.

NARRATOR. Anyway. Kamala had this crazy dream that one
day she would save the world like the super heroes she
admired.

KAMALA. Like Captain Marvel! And Iron Man. Wait,
what's wrong with wanting to save the world?

NARRATOR. *(to* **KAMALA***)* Kamala, let's be real. It was a
crazy dream.

KAMALA. Maybe. Until one day—

NARRATOR. Hey, who's the narrator here?

KAMALA. Oh, was that rude? I just thought—sorry.

NARRATOR. *(back to the audience)* Until one strange day—

KAMALA. *(excited)* There was this weird Terrigen Mist all over Jersey City and it turns out I have an Inhuman gene and it got activated and so now I have these polymorphic powers. And it's sooo cool! So I can change in size and I have super strength and I heal really fast, especially when I have a gyro and fries after a fight, and now what's really freaking awesome is I can run around town and—

NARRATOR. Ahem.

KAMALA. Oh, you're still here?

NARRATOR. Real super heroes have narrators, Kamala. With big booming voices.

KAMALA. I guess so.

NARRATOR. I'm trying to help you here.

KAMALA. Just not sure I need your help, you know? Since I'm the one with the super powers.

NARRATOR. Let me just wrap this up, okay? Acting jobs are hard to come by. I'm trying to break into the biz. You understand, right?

KAMALA. *(taken aback)* Oh, okay. Sure. Go ahead.

NARRATOR. *(booming voice again)* And now Jersey City is home to a daring young super hero who will stop at nothing to fight for justice. Who is she, you ask? Why has no one ever heard of her? Why does she have no real fans?

KAMALA. Okay, I think that's... that's enough.

NARRATOR. Why, she is none other than...

> **(KAMALA** *throws off her sweater to reveal her Ms. Marvel costume, striking a pose.)*

The Magnificent! Ms.! Marvel!

> **(KAMALA** *drops the pose.)*